Ojiichan's Gift

Written by
Chieri Uegaki

Illustrated by
Genevieve Simms

Kids Can Press

When Mayumi van Horton was
born, her grandfather built her a garden.
   It sat behind a tidy brown house nearly
halfway around the world, and it was unlike
any other garden she knew.

There were no tulips or daffodils or daisies; no carrots or cabbages or peas.

Ojiichan had made the garden out of stones — big ones, little ones and ones in between. Some reminded Mayumi of turtles. Others stood like mountains, rugged and tall.

Around the border, Ojiichan had planted pine and maple, boxwood and bamboo. And in just the right spot, by a stone lantern and a persimmon tree, was a sheltered bench where Ojiichan and Mayumi would share *onigiri bento* packed in a lacquered box.

Every summer, Mayumi spent two months with Ojiichan, and with each year, her ability to care for the garden grew.

She learned that moss on a rock was a gift of time, not to be washed away with a hose.

That weeding was more pleasant in the morning.

And that clipping shrubs to look like clouds
was the best of all reasons to prune.

Raking gravel, though, was what Mayumi enjoyed most.
She loved how the tiny rocks chattered as they passed
through the rake's wooden teeth.

She loved the different patterns she could make — wavy,
zigzag and straight. But rings, like ripples in a pond, were her
favorite.

And when she was done, Mayumi and Ojiichan would
sit and enjoy the results of her efforts in happy silence.

Often, when Mayumi was back home in her narrow house, listening to the clamor of traffic outside, she would wish for the sounds she heard at Ojiichan's — the rustle of leaves or the creak of a bough or a twittering bird.

At those times, Mayumi would open up the tin that held the souvenirs from her visits: leaves she'd pressed in a book until they dried, as delicate as dragonfly wings; tiny pinecones, still springy between her fingertips; a smooth black stone that, when warmed in her hand, helped her to remember.

Then, one summer, everything changed.

Mayumi noticed the differences as soon as she arrived. Things in the house that used to shine were dusty and dull. In the garden, shrubs and trees were overgrown, and dead leaves and needles littered the ground. Everything looked left alone.

She understood now that what her parents had told her was true. Ojiichan could not live here anymore.

Later, in Ojiichan's room, Mayumi tried to smile while she showed him photos from the school year. Birdsong wafted in on a green-scented breeze.

Mayumi looked out at her garden.

"*Hai*," Ojiichan said. "It's been waiting for you, *Mayumi-chan*."

After lunch, while Ojiichan napped, Mayumi went into the garden and walked out onto the gravel. As she stared at the rock that towered over every rock around it, the tight bud of feeling that had been in her chest all morning suddenly burst open, and with a rush, she put her hands on the rock, braced her feet in the dirt beneath and gave a mighty shove.

When nothing happened, Mayumi turned around and leaned back, knees bent. She pushed as hard as she could, wanting the rock to give, and if it did, she was going to push and push and push until the thing toppled down.

But the rock didn't budge. Not even a little.
Mayumi kicked the ground hard, spraying
gravel everywhere. She kicked again and again,
not caring, until a rock ricocheted back and hit
her on the face. She froze, and as she noticed
the mess she'd made, she put a hand to her
cheek and sagged to the ground.

After a while, Mayumi stood up and began raking because it was something useful that she could do. And as she slowly raked the gravel back in place, stooping now and then to pick up a stray leaf or to pocket a shiny pebble, a tiny idea took root.

The next morning, while her parents packed up the house, Mayumi knocked on Ojiichan's door.

"Ah, *Mayumi-chan*," he said. "Is it lunch already?"

Mayumi walked to where he sat and held out the lacquered *bento* box.

"This feels heavier than *onigiri*," Ojiichan said as he took it from her. He grinned. "What are you feeding me? Maybe … mud pie?"

Mayumi smiled and shook her head.

Ojiichan set the box on his lap and, after a moment, he lifted the lid.

"Now I've made *you* a garden," Mayumi said.
Ojiichan took her hand and gripped it tight.
"*Arigato, Mayumi-chan*," he said. "*Honto ni arigato.*
Thank you very much."

Back home, Mayumi unpacked her suitcase and set aside several small bags. Then she took out her tin and emptied it of her treasures.

The sandy gravel went in first, followed by stones of various sizes, placed just so.

She added a pinecone next, and then a leaf, before patting the gravel flat.

Then, using her pinkie as a rake, Mayumi
carefully made smooth, even rings around the
three largest rocks. And though the garden was
much smaller, and the sound was much softer, if
she closed her eyes and listened, she was certain
she could still hear the pebbles' soothing chatter.

In memory of Aiko and Alexander's Ojiichan, and for those who make gardens, wherever and however they can — C.U.

The Japanese words in this story are:

bento *(ben-TOH)*: a single serving meal (usually lunch) packaged in a portable container; also may refer to the box or container itself

-chan *(chan)*: a suffix that, when attached to the end of a person's name, expresses affection or familiarity

hai *(hi)*: yes

honto ni arigato *(hon-toh NEE ah-ree-gah-toh)*: a phrase meaning "thank you very much"

Ojiichan *(Oh-JEE-chan)*: the informal, familiar version of Ojiisan *(Oh-JEE-san)*, which means grandfather; similar to "Granddad" or "Grandpa" in English

onigiri *(oh-NEE-ghee-ree)*: small balls or triangles of rice, often filled with a pickled or salty filling, and usually wrapped in dried seaweed

Text © 2019 Chieri Uegaki
Illustrations © 2019 Genevieve Simms

Kids Can Press gratefully acknowledges the financial support of the Government of Ontario, through the Ontario Media Development Corporation; the Ontario Arts Council; the Canada Council for the Arts; and the Government of Canada for our publishing activity.

Published in Canada and the U.S. by Kids Can Press Ltd.
25 Dockside Drive, Toronto, ON M5A 0B5

Kids Can Press is a Corus Entertainment Inc. company

www.kidscanpress.com

The artwork in this book was rendered in watercolor on paper.
The text is set in Arno Pro.

Edited by Yasemin Uçar and Debbie Rogosin
Designed by Marie Bartholomew

Printed and bound in Malaysia in 10/2018 by Tien Wah Press (Pte.) Ltd.

CM 19 0 9 8 7 6 5 4 3 2 1

Library and Archives Canada Cataloguing in Publication

Uegaki, Chieri, author
    Ojiichan's gift / written by Chieri Uegaki ; illustrated by Genevieve Simms.

ISBN 978-1-77138-963-1 (hardcover)

I. Simms, Genevieve, illustrator II. Title.

PS8591.E32O44 2019   jC813'.6   C2018-902092-X

FSC
www.fsc.org
MIX
Paper from responsible sources
FSC® C012700